GHOSTS REVISITED

William P. Robertson

The tales in this book come from local folklore, friends' testimonies, and internet research. They are as factual as the author could make them although other versions are sometimes told.

Published by **BookBaby**
www.bookbaby.com

CONTENTS

CREDITS

The stories and most of the photographs in *Ghosts Revisited* first appeared in the *Ghosts, Ghosts II*, and *Ghosts III* photo books written by William P. Robertson.

All antique doll photos are by Diane Schuler while Robert Daveant provided the photographs accompanying "The Bergen House" story. On page 59 is a public domain picture of Al Capone. The Eastern State Penitentiary photo on page 61 is courtesy of Booth Kates from Pixaby. All other pics were shot by William P. Robertson.

A special thanks goes out to David Cox for creating the eerie cover. David may be contacted at dlcox1972@gmail.com.

LUKE THE SPOOK

In the fall of 1968, hysteria swept through Bradford, Pennsylvania after a ghost was sighted repeatedly at the Luke Tomb in Willow Dale Cemetery on West Washington Street. Police swore it was "boys in sheets" playing pranks when WKBW Television from Buffalo, New York sent a crew to investigate. A scared Bradford High football guard had another version to tell after a close encounter with Luke the Spook. He said the ghost was visible from the waist up and dressed in a tuxedo with a flower in its lapel. When it floated closer and beckoned to the brawny athlete, his legs melted out from beneath him. To escape, he crawled away on all fours like a dog. He had gone to the graveyard to harass parkers but suffered a harrowing experience instead!

THE CATHERINE SWAMP

The Catherine Swamp is an eerie place. Located at the head of Five Mile Brook near Clermont, Pennsylvania, it is bordered by dark rooms of hemlocks, scabby-barked cherry trees, and beech thickets whose orange leaves rattle like bones in the wind. According to legend, an immigrant girl got lost there one Christmas Eve while picking ground pine for a family wreath. A blizzard swept down on her, and she froze to death in the swirling snow. When her corpse was discovered by trappers near the swamp bearing her name, Catherine's eyes were locked in terror. Locals swear that her cries for help can still be heard echoing from the night woods today.

THE BOGERT HOUSE

The Bogert House was built in Ridgway, Pennsylvania in 1879 and served as a hotel until 1990 when it was gutted by fire on Super Bowl Sunday. It was named after one of its original owners, P.F. Bogert. The hotel was famous for its lavish barroom filled with ornate turn of the century furnishings. In its heyday, it contained a restaurant, thirty-one rooms, and eleven apartments. What isn't listed in its history is the number of lodgers who disappeared under mysterious circumstances. . .

THE HINSDALE HOUSE

Located at 3830 McMahon Road on a desolate hilltop near the village of Hinsdale, New York, the Dandy House is over a hundred years old and inhabited by age-old spirits. Built near an Indian burial ground just 250 feet from the home, blood has been seen gushing from the earth there. This cemetery reputedly inters 1,100 Senecas who were killed by their own tribe for committing evil. Often, the Dandys heard a chorus of disembodied voices echoing from the nearby woods as if performing a cleansing ritual.

Equally disturbing, the family watched smoky air in the kitchen transform into a huge gray wolf. When the beast leaped straight through a wooden door, the Iroquois word for "Leave!" was plainly heard. Then, Shadow People were seen leering in the window. After the Dandys went outside to investigate, the same faces were

10

looking out at them from the living room as lights flashed on and off.

Other ghosts were present, as well. A young, dark-haired lady was seen walking by the pond. Could she have been the woman hung from a tree out front? Then, apparitions in long gowns began appearing with startling frequency both in and out of the house. They well could have been the victims of a deranged innkeeper who murdered travelers while the dwelling served as a way station for stagecoaches.

From the time Phil Dandy, his wife Clara, and their three children moved into the house in July 1973, they were beset by dark forces. Lights turned on and off by themselves, the kitchen stove went haywire while cooking dinner, rooms got icy cold in August, and pounding and dragging noises echoed from the attic. One day they heard the slamming of a window and smashing glass. When they scrambled to look in the bedroom from which the noise issued, all the windows were in place.

Then, the haunting grew violent! After a lamp flew across the room at one of the daughters, the death card, the ace of spades, was found on the floor in her room. A few days later, two of the children woke up with burn marks covering their bodies. This prompted the family to enlist Father Alphonsus Trabold of St. Bonaventure to perform an exorcism on April 13, 1975. As he conducted his ceremony, moans and wails echoed through the house until all grew deathly still. Three months later, though, the evil forces renewed their attacks. The Dandys were eventually forced to move.

HALTON BABY CEMETERY

Halton hugs the shore of the Clarion River in Elk County Pennsylvania. In 1908 a plague swept through the village decimating its baby population. The children were buried across the river on an eerie hillside. Night photos clearly capture their ghosts. Neighbor kids leave toys for the phantom babies to play with. And then there's the dead caretaker who follows you back to your car. . .

RALPH CROSSMIRE

The ghost of Ralph Crossmire haunts the Old Jail Museum operated by the McKean County Historical Society in Smethport, Pennsylvania. Crossmire was tried and convicted of bludgeoning his mother to death with a stout piece of wood. After a death machine was erected in front of his basement cell, he was hung on December 14, 1893.

Many, including the sheriff, thought Crossmire was innocent. The evidence against him was circumstantial, there were no witnesses, and he was working in Mt. Jewett at the time.

According to the museum manager, the ghost of Ralph Crossmire is more of a practical joker than a malicious spirit. One morning, her car keys disappeared from the middle of her desk, and she tore the place apart looking for them. She found the keys dangling from a lamp near the front entrance after Ralph returned them at closing time. She also remembered Ralph taking a photo of the 1930 Port Allegany baseball team from a locked display case. The picture showed up the next day perched atop the fire alarm system in the basement.

THE LIGHTNING HOUSE

Driving north from Bradford, Pennsylvania on Seaward Avenue in the 1960s, one saw the fire-blackened sides of the Lightning House loom from the upper side of the road at the New York State Line. Some said the structure was struck often by thunderbolts, causing it to catch fire numerous times. A small boy, whose family lived there *briefly*, had another tale to tell. One night just after he had gone to bed, a tall, thin man appeared on his bedroom threshold. The figure had an incredibly wan complexion and was dressed in a dark suit and top hat. When he tipped his hat in greeting, his bald head glowed like lit coals. Yes, the house was inhabited by a poltergeist—the true reason for the many fires!

OLD FORT NIAGARA

Old Fort Niagara was originally built by the French in 1726 at the mouth of the Niagara River near present-day Youngstown, New York. After a nineteen-day siege, the British captured the stronghold during the French and Indian War and held it through the American Revolution. The United States occupied the fort at the outbreak of the War of 1812.

Besides being an impressive historic site, Old Fort Niagara is haunted by a French officer named Henri Le Clerc. He was murdered by a rival while quarreling over an Indian maiden. The killer cut off the dead officer's head, tossed it in Lake Ontario, and stuffed the rest of the body down a well. To this day, the ghost of Henri Le Clerc wanders about the fort castle looking for his head.

THE DEVIL'S DEN

Over 7,000 men were killed at the Battle of Gettysburg that raged from July 1-3, 1863 in Adams County Pennsylvania. With so many violent and untimely deaths, no wonder the battlefield is a hotbed of ghostly activity.

One of the most haunted sites at Gettysburg is the Devil's Den located off Crawford Avenue south of town. At the end of Houck's Ridge, the boulder-strewn hill made a perfect fort for Confederate snipers.

A barefoot Rebel in ragged clothes and a floppy hat still makes surprise appearances amid the rocks today. After drawling, "What you're looking for is over there," he vanishes! The ghost is dressed like the Texas soldiers who captured the Devil's Den with great loss of life.

THE NORTH HALL GHOST

A freshman music student named Sarah committed suicide by leaping down the central stairwell of North Hall Dormitory at Mansfield Normal School either in the World War I era or the 1930s. In one version, the girl receives a letter from the Western Front saying her lover was killed in action. Overcome with grief, she kills herself to join him in the hereafter. In another, a pregnant Sarah is jilted by the father of her child and takes her own life rather than face the shame accompanying her lost virtue. A third account even involves a Ouija board that tells the freshman to jump!

Mansfield is a renowned music school, and North Hall has a practice room located on the top floor. Many students have heard melodies resonating from there only to find it empty upon entering. Adding to Sarah's legend is the testimony of a revered professor who reported seeing her spectral face staring at him from an upper story window.

A freshman from Bradford, Pennsylvania had a real scare at the expense of Sarah in 1968. In those days, Mansfield was called a "suitcase college," because most students went home every weekend. One Friday, the girl found herself completely alone on the fifth floor. She was about to turn in for the night when she heard footsteps. Strangely, the footfalls stopped before every room, and the doors creaked open one-by-one as the intruder proceeded up the hall. She thought at first it was Lefty, the one-armed security guard, making his rounds. That was until no one knocked to check on her!

Mustering up her courage, the girl finally tiptoed to her door, unlocked it, and peeked out into the corridor. There, floated a misty figure in a baggy-sleeved dress. Her abundant hair was straight on the top and curly down the back of her neck. She wore high-topped shoes and dark stockings. Turning, she fixed the coed with a dreamy smile. Then, she opened her arms and beckoned with both hands before slowly fading from view. After that, the girl from Bradford fled campus on weekends like everyone else!

HAUNTED STRAUGHN AUDITORIUM

Straughn Auditorium has hosted many prestigious events and celebrities since it opened at Mansfield State Teachers College in 1927. The inaugurations of several campus presidents have taken place there along with professional and student productions of *Twelfth Night, South Pacific, Brigadoon,* and *Barefoot in the Park.* Famous pop bands have performed in the hall, as well, including Bread, the Grass Roots, and the Vogues. Tom Wolfe, Dr. Benjamin Spock, and Muhammad Ali are just a few of the famous people who have spoken at the 1,100-seat facility that continues to resonate with gifted voices from the national scene today.

One guest who remains unannounced, however, is the giant shadow figure that lurks in the balcony and the descending stairwell. According to a media services worker who saw it,

21

the ghost is at least seven feet tall. The workman was adjusting some lights on stage around 11:30 p.m. when he first noticed a dark silhouette above him and yelled an unanswered "Hello." Thinking it was someone associated with the theater, he went back to work until a strange feeling crept over him. Glancing up, the technician then saw the tall phantom and watched it wide-eyed for several seconds. Finally, it glided across the balcony, hesitated for an instant, and then shot down the stairs. When it passed by the wall lights during its descent, they were deadened by its shadow. Later, a spooked custodian spotted the figure twice in the very same spot.

A lady who rented the theater for a school play was scared next. Working late on last-minute changes to her script, she spied the gaunt specter slouched in a chair and left screaming. When ghost hunters were called in to investigate, an EVP of a frightened voice cried out, "Don't hurt me!" Another immediately uttered in a stern tone, "You can never tell anyone what happened." What did happen to raise these spirits in Straughn Hall is anyone's guess!

THE PINK HOUSE

The Pink House sits on the corner of West State Street and Brooklyn Avenue, a block down from the high school in Wellsville, New York. It could just as well be named the "Heartbreak House," because of the loveless marriage Frances Farnum was forced into by her father with E.B. Hall, the rich owner of the mansion. After his wife drown herself in the fountain to escape her grief, Hall soon married Frances' sister, Antoinette, and they returned from their honeymoon with a newborn daughter. When the daughter also drown in the fountain two years later, Antoinette thought the spirit of Frances took out her revenge on the child. Two mournful ghosts now roam the grounds, weeping endlessly.

THE HITCHHIKER

A lady barber often tells her customers an unsettling tale. At a previous job, she worked until one a.m. and then drove home through Allegany, New York. One night in a steady drizzle, she saw a tall man wearing a slicker hitchhiking along the road. Although she didn't stop to pick him up, she felt a strange presence enter her car. Glancing quickly from the corner of her eye, she saw the fellow in the raincoat slumped in the passenger seat. Her hands began shaking on the wheel, but somehow she kept control of her vehicle. Staring straight ahead, she sped down the black highway listening to the wipers slap the raindrops from her windshield. The ghost never spoke or threatened her. When she drove past the Limestone Cemetery near the New York State Line, he simply vanished. He was hitching a ride home is all. Perhaps from where he had died in a car wreck.

GOODLEBURG CEMETERY

The name "Goodleburg" means hill of the ghouls, and the cemetery near Wales, New York lives up to that billing. Visitors have had many scary experiences in this desolate burying place. Commonly seen are a dead mother in white, black hellhounds with glowing red eyes, and a low-hanging fog that follows ghost hunters. There are also the cries of babies, crawling baby ghosts, and baby handprints left on dewy car windows.

The scariest legend, though, centers upon an abortion doctor who lived across the road. He deposited the infants he killed in hastily dug graves throughout the cemetery. The mothers who died during his gristly procedures were dumped in a nearby pond. The doctor's ghost began appearing in the late 1800s after he hung himself out of guilt.

Goodleburg has become a dangerous place since vandals knocked down most of the tombstones. The spirits are angry, so be careful not to further desecrate their home. Injuries are known to happen here.

ALLEGANY COUNTY POORHOUSE

The Allegany County Poorhouse opened in 1831 on County Road 2 east of Angelica, New York and housed impoverished and mentally ill residents. It was built on a farm of 180 acres where healthy inmates worked to provide food and an income for the institution. The original two-story building was made of stone but was poorly ventilated. It contained seventeen wards that were supervised by two male keepers. There was no bathtub or even a bathroom. Equally awful, the paupers slept on straw pallets, often with lice as their bedfellows.

The insane were barbarously treated and confined to filthy cells with a ball and chain. Unruly inmates received a "tanning." In short, the keeper flogged them with a rawhide whip until they became docile. The treatment of children was bad, too. It was common for kids to be tortured by their peers, mentally disturbed adults, or sadistic staff members. Finally, in 1876, all children over the age of three were sent to foster homes or orphanages to solve this problem.

In succeeding years, four new buildings were constructed to accommodate more needy individuals. The first housed the administrative offices, the inmates' dining room and kitchen, and the employees' sleeping quarters. It was connected to the women's dormitory by a fifty-foot passageway. In the back was the men's concrete dorm while the superintendent and his family occupied a home out front.

In March of 1923, in what was described as "the most horrible event in the history of Allegany County," this second poorhouse burned to the ground. The blaze started in the boiler room beneath the administration building and quickly spread after a loud explosion. Four bed-ridden women and a night fireman were roasted alive by the unrelenting flames. Others escaped by jumping out upstairs windows. Among them was a large woman who was severely hurt in her fall. Too heavy to carry, she was rolled over and over until safe from the scalding heat.

Only the men's dormitory escaped destruction, and a year later, work on three fireproof structures was begun. This safer version of the poorhouse remained open until 1965. It has since deteriorated into the horrid condition captured in the accompanying photos.

As documented by many investigators, inside the complex are spooky rooms filled with curiosities. One chamber is completely littered with old newspapers while another is a graveyard for wrecked pianos. Swaying rocking chairs, a broken tricycle, and rotting sofas make the place eerie, too.

Visitors have the sensation of being followed, but no one answers the oft-asked question, "Is anyone there?" Even creepier is the random sound of slamming doors. Were they shut by the wind gusting through broken windows? Or by the hands of spectral lunatics?

BOLDT CASTLE

George C. Boldt made a fortune as proprietor of the Waldorf-Astoria in New York City and Philadelphia's Bellevue-Stratford. In 1899, he began construction of a fairy tale house to honor his beloved wife, Louise. He selected Heart Island in the St. Lawrence River at Alexandria Bay, New York for its location.

Over the next four years, George poured 2.5 million dollars into his replica of an old German castle that contained 120 rooms and was 60 stories high. Also, he commissioned the building of a yacht house and a children's playhouse. The latter included a stage, a music room, and a bowling alley.

Boldt wanted everything finished by Valentine's Day of 1905 as a romantic gift for Louise. His wife, though, died unexpectedly of heart failure in January 1904. George was so grief-stricken by her death that he stopped work on the almost completed castle and didn't set foot on Heart Island again. Ironically, he never saw the architectural treasure his workmen had built in the name of love.

Today, Mrs. Boldt's spirit roams the premises watching the restoration of her cherished home. Her footsteps are heard in suddenly chilly halls, and the light she shines from tower windows has been seen by many.

PURE-SIL

In Bradford, Pennsylvania a foreboding brick building sat along East Main Street down by the B&O railroad tracks. Crisscrossed with ivy that turned bloodred in the fall, it served over the years as a silk mill, a skating rink, and a silicon factory. In its latter capacity, it was known as Venton, Pensilco, and then Pure-Sil before falling victim to the wrecking ball.

Nightshift employees of Pure-Sil found the place quite unsettling. Machines in every department would simultaneously crash, causing curses and delays. Cold breezes would engulf walkers in the hall, too, even when doors were shut tight. Some swore they heard the cries of phantom skaters accompany these gusts.

One night, the quality control room grew frigid with the air conditioner *off*. The technician told the invading spirit to leave in the name of Jesus Christ. When it refused to budge, the QC man fled instead.

What every worker feared most, though, was being sent to the North End to fetch equipment from storage. Lurking there were rats as big as cats that showed no fear of humans.

GURNSEY HOLLOW CEMETERY

Frewsburg, New York, located in the dense woods of Chautauqua County, was populated in the 1800s by many Irish immigrants. These townspeople were devout Catholics and *more* than a little superstitious. Among them lived a seven-year-old girl named Sarah who put everyone's nerves on edge. The odd, retarded girl was thought to be possessed or even a practitioner of witchcraft. One day, she got the citizens so riled that they chased her from the village. The girl sought escape down Gurnsey Road with her pursuers hot on her heels. She ran, spewing gibberish, until reaching a trail that veered off to the right. In a panic, she took it, only to become trapped inside a remote graveyard surrounded by an iron fence. When she reached a tall cross at the back of the grounds, she collapsed, whimpering like an animal. The furious mob closed in and pummeled her with stones until she quit crying. Sarah was buried where she was murdered and her ghost unleashed. Visitors can still hear her giggles as she pokes them and pulls their hair. Her phantom footsteps skip and jump and play while moans and heavy thumps echo from the nearly forest at Gurnsey Hollow Cemetery.

KANE COMMUNITY HOSPITAL

Nurses at the Community Hospital in Kane, Pennsylvania swear the facility is haunted. Through a public fund campaign spearheaded by W.S. Calderwood, the original brick structure was built in 1929 and remained unchanged until 1972 when a major upgrade was completed to meet the town's growing needs. Located at 4372 Route 6, the hospital now goes by the name UPMC Kane.

The old wing is where most ghostly activity occurs. Seen frequently is a phantom gentleman dressed in a three-piece suit. He stands with his back and one raised foot braced against the wall. Also observed is a woman in a long white nightgown who floats across the hall from one room to another and back again. Then, there's an IV pump that turns itself on. It begins to beep feverishly even though it's not plugged in!

Sitting at the nurses' station at night can be creepy, too. The on-duty RN often catches movement out of the corner of her eye as though a person rushed past. When she turns her head, there is never anyone there. Equally disturbing, nurses have had someone speak their names only to find themselves alone in the hall. And finally there's the black shadow figure in the parking lot that causes nurses to hustle to their cars after the nightshift is over.

THE BARBER HOUSE

The Barber House is located at the corner of Short Tract and Oakland Roads in Portage, New York. Also known as Chestnut Place, it was completed in the late 1800s by John Failing Barber, a successful businessman and farmer. He had purchased the mansion from his brother-in-law, Nathaniel Alward, and the family referred to it as "the house on the hill."

Barber, who was married three times, had impeccable taste, and his new residence was beautifully designed. It had plate glass windows, a marble bathroom, three ornate fireplaces, curly maple doors, and a spiral staircase built of cherry. There were fifteen rooms and nine closets, all amply furnished.

Barber's granddaughter, Ethel Bennett, and her husband were the last family members to live at Chestnut Place before moving to Alden, New York in 1920. After that, the home was occupied by Robert Gath, who kept it in pristine condition. A string of less-caring tenants followed, including a Mrs. Peaks. She ran a cat refuge there until 1994.

Now, bats hibernate in several rooms, and a ghostly, white-haired woman has been seen leering from upper story windows. The property was recently posted to keep out trespassers for their own well-being. According to one neighbor, the floors are unsafe to walk on, and no one wants to haul bodies from the basement!

TOTTEN HOLLOW

Totten Hollow is located off South Kendall Avenue near Bradford, Pennsylvania. It's the home of a working farm, oil field relics, and a haunted house. The house sits at the end of Totten Lane above the school bus turnaround. Different entities have been seen there over the years. When an elderly lady occupied the residence, a playful ghost named Oscar kept her company. He didn't try to frighten her; he just enjoyed playing pranks. His favorite trick was moving things from their rightful place for fun. After the woman passed away, Oscar hasn't been seen since. Soon after, though, he was replaced by a spirit dressed in a long black coat. During his tenure, doors would open and close, furniture would move, and the piano would play by itself. Later, the house was inhabited by a peculiar mother and her equally odd daughter. These ladies were so strange, that while they were alive, they scared everyone in the neighborhood!

FALL BROOK

In 1862, Fall Brook was a thriving coal town of 14,000 residents. Located in the heart of Tioga County Pennsylvania, it was connected by railroad to Corning, New York where its coal was shipped to the Erie Canal. The town boasted of a hotel and numerous blacksmith shops and boarding houses. It was also the victim of a smallpox outbreak in the winter of 1871 that claimed the lives of many children. Likewise, fires were a problem. In May 1872, a conflagration swept through the surrounding woods and would have engulfed the village if the entire population hadn't pitched in to fight it. Another fire burnt down the hotel in 1899, the year Fall Brook was abandoned after the mines had run dry.

All that exists of Fall Brook today are a few foundations and a field of blighted tombstones encompassed by thick trees. Caskets are rising in the graveyard and form mounds close to the earth's surface. Many of the stones are broken and include engravings of clasped hands, ascending doves, and fingers pointing skyward. Considering the deplorable condition of this site, it's no wonder ghost stories have sprung from the surrounding region.

It's true, though, that visitors have seen dark figures and have felt like they were being watched. A woman's agonizing scream has also been heard bursting from the woods, and a team of investigators captured an EVP of a voice crying, "Help me!" Another ghost hunter witnessed a black shadow walk through a headstone and felt cold spots in different locales. Then, there's that foreboding birch that sits at the back of the cemetery. Carved in jagged letters in its rough bark are the words, "Leave Now." It's a message that makes one's skin crawl even in broad daylight.

THE LEGEND OF OLE BULL

Parts of Northcentral Pennsylvania have become known as the Black Forest, because the trees are so thick that sunlight can't penetrate them. This is where world-renown concert violinist, Ole Bornemann Bull, decided to establish a colony for his fellow Norwegians in September 1852. His homeland had fallen under Swedish rule due to the decision of the 1815 Vienna Congress, and he looked to find freedom in America. The price he was to pay for that liberty was even too much for his deep pockets.

Ole Bull built the settlements of New Bergen, Oleanna, New Norway, and Valhalla in Kettle Creek Valley near Coudersport that resembled the steep landscapes of his youth. He purchased 11,144 acres from John Cowan of Williamsport, and by January 1853, the settlers had erected two water mills, a steam sawmill, and a new school. Bull also began constructing a towered mountain castle that was made of lumber.

The woods were incredibly dense, and the colonists struggled to clear just enough of them to plant crops the next spring. In May, their dreams came crashing down when the Stewardson family from Philadelphia arrived and demanded that the Norwegians leave Kettle Creek. They were the rightful owners of the land, not the deceitful broker, John Cowan.

When Ole Bull learned that he'd been swindled, he went a little crazy. He wandered off into the forest madly playing his Stradivarius for the rattlesnakes, panthers, and bears. He appeared at a tavern several days later with his hair disheveled and a wild look on his face. After a few stiff drinks, he stumbled off to his unfinished manor where he planned another tour to recoup his losses. The other colonists moved to Wisconsin to live with fellow Scandinavians.

It is rumored that the ghost of Ole Bull has returned to his beloved mountaintop in the state park bearing his name. On dark, stormy nights, haunted music floats from the ruins of his castle and is heard by scared campers below. Children creep deeper into their sleeping bags to escape the strains of violin while adults play deaf or take longer pulls from their liquor bottles.

SENECA BOGLES

Between the Red House and Quaker exits on Route 86 near Salamanca, New York, sits an extremely haunted section of the Seneca Indian Reservation. Most prominent is a hemlock-ridden mountain that towers above Bay State Run. Known as Ga'Hai Hill, it's where many legendary creatures roam. Talking animals, a white bear, and deer that walk upright on their hind legs have been seen in the enchanted woods. Hikers often return pasty-faced after hearing spooky tom-toms beating on the summit. Overwhelmed by the evil atmosphere of the place, the average camper flees from there halfway through the night.

Another eerie area is the Witches' Walk that runs along the foot of Ga'Hai Hill near the Allegheny River. It's so haunted that only witches and wizards dare go there after sunset. It was the scene of a great battle between the Seneca and Erie tribes many years ago. The ghosts of the slain warriors relive their bloody deaths as they wail and smite each other when the moon rises.

Witch Lights are seen there, too. These are luminous spheres resembling glowing footballs that float above the ground. Twisted faces peer out of them as they sail past in the gloom. They convey witches from place to place when the evil ones are weary of traveling on foot.

The Seneca bogeyman known as High Hat also creeps about the swamps near the Witches' Walk. He is a cannibalistic giant with a lust for children's flesh. He has a gruff voice and a mouth full of sharp teeth. Like a deranged Abraham Lincoln in a stovepipe hat, this monster captures unsuspecting kids. He devours them on the spot or hangs them in thorn trees to eat later.

The Pennsylvania Railroad used to run through the Witches' Walk. On several occasions, an engineer braked his train to keep from hitting dark figures tramping the tracks ahead. As his locomotive screeched to a halt, the wayfarers vanished! Then, there was the night train that stopped due to mechanical failure. After the conductor got off to investigate, he was never seen or heard from again.

DUNKIRK LIGHTHOUSE

On a point jutting out into Lake Erie near Dunkirk, New York, sits a lighthouse that's famous for more than its powerful Fresnel lens that can be seen through darkness, fog, or mist for twenty-seven miles. Originally built in 1826, it was later reconstructed to include a sixty-one foot stone tower and a brick keeper's house that remain standing today. The property on which they were built is where the first shot of the War of 1812 was fired when the British warship, *Lady Provost*, was driven off by local militia. The first Civil War soldier killed in action is buried here, too. The spirit of Corporal Cyrus Jones of Dunkirk has been seen by many.

Other resident ghosts are the former owners of the military artifacts housed in the Veterans Museum at the keeper's house. Some dead keepers have hung around, as well, and William Sinfield, who ran the lighthouse during the Civil War, appears often. There are also phantom children present. They are believed to be victims of a fire that enveloped the steamship *Erie* in 1841 and claimed the lives of 150 passengers and crew just offshore from Dunkirk.

The most famous ghost, though, is named Charlie. He drown while trying to save some youngsters who were caught in the surf. He is very protective of the property and told the current caretaker to leave when he showed up unexpectedly one April to shut off the water. A creepy doll that's nearly 100 years old provides chills, too. It moves by itself and plays with a ball and rattle that change positions from where they sat the night before. Equally spooky is the windup Victrola that Charlie allows visitors to play only if kids are in the room.

HOTEL CONNEAUT

Hotel Conneaut began operating in 1903 at the Conneaut Lake Resort in Crawford County Pennsylvania. Dubbed "the Crown Jewel of Conneaut Park," it contains 150 quaint rooms, many of which are haunted!

The scariest chamber, by far, is 321 where water faucets turn on by themselves, beds become rumpled after the maid remakes them, and whispered conversations disturb sleepers. The ghost bride Elizabeth spent her last hours there before her honeymoon was permanently canceled when lightning stuck the hotel roof on April 29, 1943. The resulting fire spread quickly, and billowing smoke added to the confusion. Her husband, thinking Elizabeth had already escaped, looked for her outside. She, meanwhile, searched the burning building for him and was fried to a crisp for her efforts. Visitors still see her wispy figure roaming the third floor to this day. She is clothed in her wedding gown, and the distinct scent of jasmine is detected as she passes down the hall.

Actually, most paranormal activity occurs on the third floor. After the maid cleans and locks Rooms 304, 310, 311, 317, 331, 335, 339, and 340, the occupants often find their doors wide open when they return from downstairs. Guests in Rooms 312 and 329 are wakened at night by a ferocious scratching at their doors. They find deep lacerations in the wood the next morning and generally check out early. And then there's 302, also known as the "Round Room." Families feel faint while occupying it and experience sudden drops in the temperature. They are also unnerved by a mirror that turns by itself!

Ghostly children are observed at Hotel Conneaut, too. First, there's the lost little boy who is looking for his mother. His name is Michael, and he frequently climbs deckchairs to peer in the first floor windows. Angelina, on the other hand, wanders the halls seeking someone to play with. The small girl was killed long ago while riding her tricycle. She either plunged to her death off the hotel balcony or crashed down a flight of stairs. An apparition with long blond hair can still be seen at dusk wildly pedaling her trike across the porch.

The kitchen is another haunted place. That's where a feuding chef and butcher argued furiously. Finally, after hurling knives and pans at each other, the chef dismembered the butcher in a fit of rage. An eeriness still lingers there, and windows open on their own after being nailed shut!

MAD ANTHONY WAYNE

General "Mad" Anthony Wayne was a true hero of the American Revolution. His nickname sprang from his fiery temperament and the aggressive battle tactics he used at Brandywine, Monmouth, and Stony Point. He began the war as a colonel in the 4th Pennsylvania Regiment that was sent in January 1776 to participate in the disastrous invasion of Canada. His men performed ably at the Battle of Trois-Rivieres while fighting a delaying action that allowed the beaten Continental Army to escape capture. Soon after, Wayne was appointed commander of Fort Ticonderoga.

While in charge of this important installation guarding the north-south water route from Lake Champlain, Mad Anthony displayed a less desirable aspect of his personality. It was here that he cheated on his wife, Mary Penrose, with a woman named Nancy Coates. His fascination with her didn't last long, either, and she drown herself after learning he had left her for yet another woman. Her ghost now haunts the damp stone fort and has been seen by visitors and staff alike. Nancy still waits near the gate for Wayne's arrival or dashes madly about searching for him. Her sobs have been heard by many, too, and some even claim to have seen her body floating on the waves of Lake Champlain.

Ironically, General Wayne's passing also didn't end in peaceful rest. After defeating the Miami war chief, Little Turtle, at the Battle of Fallen Timbers in 1794, Mad Anthony died from gout on his way home two years later. He was buried at Fort Presque Isle near Erie, Pennsylvania, much to the chagrin of his children.

At his daughter's request, Wayne's body was eventually exhumed, so it could be reburied in a family plot at Radnor, PA in the southeast corner of the state. When the casket was opened, though, the general's corpse was very much intact. To facilitate its transport, the flesh was scraped and boiled from his skeleton. After the flayed tissue was poured back into the original grave, the bones were sent on their way. According to legend, they were packed incorrectly, and some spilled out during the 400 mile journey. Now each year on his January 1st birthday, Mad Anthony mounts his horse and rides along Route 322 to recover his lost bones. He will not rest until they are found. Nor will anyone who sees him gallop past on the night highway.

ERIE CEMETERY

Erie Cemetery was officially opened in 1851 and is now home for over 50,000 souls. Situated downtown, it encompasses 75 acres between Cherry and Chestnut Streets. Such noteworthy citizens as Rear Admiral John Marshall Boyer, U.S. Congressman William L. Scott, and three Medal of Honor winners (Andrew P. Forbeck, Milden Henry Wilson, and William Young) are buried there. Also interred are Daniel Dobbins, who oversaw the construction of Oliver Perry's flcct during the War of 1812, and Brigadier General Strong Vincent, the hero of Little Round Top at Gettysburg.

There is an eerie side to the graveyard, too. Old oaks and hickory trees add a spooky atmosphere and appear to be gobbling up nearby tombstones. The most chills, though, are provided by a plain-looking crypt built into a Section 19 hillside. Much mystery surrounds this tomb. Although it is owned by Gertrude Brown, she was never buried there. According to cemetery records, it was G.W. Goodrich who first found his resting place in the crypt during November of 1884. Presently, there are seven residents, including a vampire!

As legend has it, an unidentified Erie man journeyed to Romania and died of consumption when he returned. After his burial in the Vampire Crypt, dead bodies were discovered within close proximity to Erie Cemetery. Each of the corpses had puncture wounds on the neck and was drained of blood. A maintenance man, who lived on the grounds, discovered the monster's secret. He padlocked the vault door, so the creature couldn't feed. Once word leaked out about the vampire, neighbors stormed the crypt, chiseled its name off the lintel, and burned the tomb black. Today, an ornate V̲ over the doorway is its only identifying mark.

Not far from the Vampire Crypt is a circle of headstones where witches are reputedly buried. This was the site of a satanic ritual that went bad. It is said that the devil himself appeared during the ceremony and dragged several of his followers screaming off to hell. In another version, Satan didn't attend the ritual. Instead, he came to collect the souls of two witches. When he touched the tombstones under which they were planted, the stones were hideously charred.

EASTERN STATE PENITENTIARY

Located at 2027 Fairmount Avenue in North Philadelphia, Eastern State Penitentiary resembles a Gothic castle with thick, stone walls; numerous towers; and gargoyles guarding the front entrance. The facility opened in 1829 and provided an alternative to overcrowded prisons filled with violence, corruption, and abuse.

At Eastern State, solitary confinement was the norm. Each prisoner had his own cell complete with a flush toilet, a water tap, hot water heating, and an attached exercise yard. In the ceiling was a skylight called the "Eye of God" that let the inmate know God was watching. It was hoped that time alone would allow a criminal to reflect on his wrongdoing and become penitent. The name "penitentiary" reflects that goal. With inmates confined in absolute silence for months on end, Eastern State soon became an insane asylum, as well. There were over fifty suicides and a dozen murders while the prison was in operation until 1971.

Despite the noble purpose of the penitentiary, rebellious prisoners were treated harshly. In winter, they were dunked in a "Water Bath" and hung outside until coated with ice. The "Mad Chair" was even worse. Sometimes for days, an inmate was strapped so tightly in it that his circulation was cut off. Amputations were later required. Then, there was the "Iron Gag" that was nothing but pure torture. The malefactor's tongue was chained to his wrist, so that any struggle would cause the tongue to rip and bleed. This was accompanied by intense pain. The most heinous offenders, though, were sent to "The Hole," an underground pit immersed in complete darkness. There was no toilet, very little food, and not much ventilation. This thin air didn't prevent the claustrophobic from screaming!

Due to overcrowding, Eastern State Penitentiary reverted to a congregate prison system in 1913, and convicts began sharing cells and communicating with each other. By the 1940s many hauntings were reported, too. Throughout the prison, footsteps, wails, whispers, tortured cries, sadistic laughter, and the opening and slamming of cell doors were heard with startling frequency. A glittering blob was also seen that appeared and disappeared in an instant. In Cellblock 12 cackling voices were detected while shadow figures darted from Cellblock 6.

Cellblock 4, however, was the most haunted place. Known for ghostly faces gleaming on the walls, it provided a real scare for locksmith, Gary Johnson, in the 1990s. He claims that a powerful force gripped him there so tightly that he couldn't move until a dark energy exploded from the cell he had just unlocked. Other employees quit without notice when confronted by similar entities.

The most famous haunting involved gangster, Al Capone, who spent eight months in Eastern State in 1929 on a concealed weapons charge. Capone was confined in the "Park Avenue Block" in a single cell furnished with homemade rugs, expensive furniture, oil paintings, and a radio. The thug received no comfort from his lavish surroundings, however, when the ghost of James Clark began visiting him nightly. He ordered Clark murdered in the St. Valentine's Day Massacre, and the vengeful spirit enacted its own kind of justice in return. The murderous

Scarface was reduced to a blubbering mess as he emitted bloodcurdling screams and shouted, "Jimmy! Jimmy! Leave me alone!" These entreaties went unheeded, for the phantom tormented Capone until his death in 1947.

THE BERGEN HOUSE

Built in 1858, the Bergen House is nestled in the sleepy countryside of Genesee County near Rochester, New York. The triangular-shaped property sits adjacent to an ancient swamp where witches allegedly held black masses. Seen often are a ghostly lady trudging up the driveway and a Peeping Tom phantom gazing in ground floor windows. Also observed is a dark figure lurking in the barn loft. This could be the serial killer who resided here in the not too distant past. He snatched kids off the Orphan Train, brutally murdered them, and disposed of their bodies by feeding them to the pigs. The barn became doubly haunted after a neighbor girl hung herself from the rafters. Pregnant and spurned by her boyfriend, she was backed into the black corner known as suicide.

Inside the house, many spirits skulk, as well. Visitors are spooked by a cranky man's growls and the disembodied voices of frightened children. Several have felt trapped by dark forces in the attic while others experienced disorientation and dread. Equally eerie, the closet in the "Blue Room" causes cameras to malfunction. It serves as a portal to the spirit world, and ghosts have been seen issuing from there to confer on the bed. The owner of the house had a bad fright in the living room, too, while hanging the portrait of a girl with a bow in her hair. When the girl's eyes moved and her lips smiled maliciously, the owner dropped the picture like it was hot. *Somehow*, it escaped harm after crashing violently to the floor.

THE GHOSTS OF BARCLAY MOUNTAIN

Grim Barclay Mountain is located in the wilderness of Bradford County Pennsylvania and towers 2,041 feet above sea level. Coal was originally discovered there by Absalom Carr while hunting for deer. At first, the coal was transported downhill on sleds and taken to Towanda where blacksmith, Jared Leavenworth, began using it. To supply other blacksmiths in Pennsylvania and Southern New York, the Mason and Cash mine was opened. Roads were soon carved through the woods, and wagons rumbled across them to carry coal to market.

It was only after the Barclay Railroad from Towanda was built in 1856, however, that the mining industry took off. In its heyday, 380,000 tons of coal were shipped annually, and Barclay became a thriving village. When the population swelled to 800, construction began on a schoolhouse, a post office, a Presbyterian church, several stores, and the freight and engine houses of the railroad. Coal was transported down the mountain then by a sophisticated incline plane rail system. Over four million tons of coal were harvested before the mines petered out in 1890. The village itself was later destroyed by a strip mining operation. All that exists of it today are a few foundations and a creepy cemetery perched on the mountain.

Coal mining was a dangerous occupation, and many workers suffered wretched demises. Some were crushed in sudden cave-ins while others, inflicted with black lung disease, slowly strangled to death. The ghosts of Barclay Cemetery aren't mournful, though. Visitors hear them whistling or exchanging pleasant greetings. Their pick axes merrily strike the ground in an eternal search for the very thing that killed them!

WILDWOOD SANITARIUM

Wildwood Sanitarium stands in a quiet neighborhood at 71 Prospect Avenue, Salamanca, New York. Established in 1906 by Dr. Henderson and Dr. Perry, it originally served up to ten patients who sought cures for drug addiction, alcoholism, or stress-related illnesses. Providing individual attention to the afflicted, the physicians used holistic treatments without drugs. Henderson and Perry also administered Osteopathy Therapy. This included chiropractic adjustments to bones and muscles to treat chronic physiological diseases. The bathhouse in the basement provided another option to relax the agitated. These practices continued to help sufferers until the facility became a tuberculosis clinic in 1923.

Today, the building is in disrepair, and pigeons coo in the broken eaves like dispossessed souls. An old ghost, complaining of rickets, roams an upper floor. Refusing to pass to the other side, the medical staff is still on call. An icy nurse will attempt to take your pulse, only to quicken it!

ABOUT THE AUTHOR

Hi, I'm Bill Robertson. I don't consider myself a spooky guy. I just like visiting haunted places and learning their history. I discovered the supernatural at an early age when my Swedish grandmother told me folktales about trolls and witches. She said that trolls would ride you to the ground and suck away your soul! My dad was extremely well-read, and he urged me in junior high to peruse the work of Edgar Allan Poe. I was especially impressed by the eerie settings Poe wove into his stories. It was the Gothic rock of the Doors, though, that hooked me on the horror genre. Their organ-mad music and tortured vocals had an irresistible appeal, as did Jim Morrison's dark imagery. Since becoming attuned to the paranormal, I've had several spooky encounters that are included in *Ghosts Revisited*. Go to **thehorrorhaven.com** for more information about my writing.

BOOKS BY WILLIAM P. ROBERTSON

Short Story Collections

Lurking in Pennsylvania (2004), *Dark Haunted Day* (2006), *Terror Time* (2009), *The Dead of Winter* (2010), *Season of Doom* (2013), *Terror Time 2nd Edition* (2013), *Stories from the Olden Days* (2015), *Misdeeds and Misadventures* (2016), *More Stories from the Olden Days* (2017), *Love That Burns* (2017), *War in the Colonies* (2018), *Fear Is Forever* (2018), *Fun in the Olden Days* (2018), *Come In* (2019).

Novels

Hayfoot, Strawfoot: The Bucktail Recruits (2002), *The Bucktails' Shenandoah March* (2002), *The Bucktails: Perils on the Peninsula* (2006), *The Bucktails' Antietam Trials* (2006), *The Battling Bucktails at Fredericksburg* (2006), *The Bucktails at the Devil's Den* (2007), *The Bucktails' Last Call* (2007), *Ambush in the Alleghenies* (2008), *Attack in the Alleghenies* (2010), *This Enchanted Land: The Saga of Dane Wulfdin* (2010), *The Bucktail Brothers of the Fighting 149th* (2011), *The Bucktail Brothers: Brave Men's Blood* (2012), *The 190th Bucktails: Catchin' Bobby Lee* (2014), *Annihilated in the Alleghenies* (2016).

Poetry Volumes

Burial Grounds (1977), *Gardez Au Froid* (1979), *Animal Comforts* (1981), *Life After Sex Life* (1983), *Waters Boil Bloody* (1990), *1066* (1992), *Hearse Verse* (1994), *The Illustrated Book of Ancient, Medieval & Fantasy Battle* Verse (1996), *Desolate Landscapes* (1997), *Bone Marrow Drive* (1997), *Ghosts of a Broken Heart* (2005), *Icicles* (2018), *Lost* (2018).

Audio Books

Gasp! (1999), *Until Death Do Impart* (2002), *Bucktail Tales* (2013).

Photo Books

*Tombstones & Shadows (2019), **Graveyards: Glorious & Ghostly* (2019), **Abandoned Dwellings* (2019), **The Pennsylvania Bucktails* (2019), **An Eye for the Eerie* (2019), **Ghosts* (2019), **Ghosts II* (2020), **Ghosts III* (2020).

E-Books

The above titles marked with a star (*) are also available in Kindle, i-Pad, and Nook e-book formats. *The Bucktail Brothers Series* combines both *The Bucktail Brothers of the Fighting 149th* and *The Bucktail Brothers: Brave Men's Blood* into one e-book.